HAZEL TOWNSON

Charlie the Champion Traveller

illustrated by PHILIPPE DUPASQUIER

First published in Great Britain 1995
by Methuen Children's Books Ltd
Published 1996 by Mammoth
an imprint of Reed International Books Ltd,
Michelin House, 81 Fulham Road, London SW3 6RB
and Auckland, Melbourne, Singapore and Toronto

ISBN 0 7497 2590 7

A CIP catalogue record for this book is available
at the British Library

Printed in Great Britain by Cox & Wyman Ltd, Reading, Berkshire

Contents

For Blanche and
Joseph Gadian

ONE

A Big Mistake

Charlie Lyle's heart sank down into his trainers. There he was, trying his hardest to please Miss Walker when, completely out of the blue, disaster struck. Miss Walker was the best teacher Charlie had ever known. Her smile of approval meant more to him than a whole weekend's television. Yet now he was about to let her down in the most spectacular way.

'Put your hands up if you've ever been away on holiday,' Miss Walker had asked. Everyone had put their hands up, including Charlie who had never been away on holiday in his life, though he did not intend to admit it.

'Good! That's all of you!' Miss Walker had smiled. 'Then we can go ahead with a very special project. I want you all to prepare a talk entitled 'My best holiday ever', then one by one, over the next few weeks, you will be expected to stand out in front of the class and deliver your talk, illustrating it, if possible, with brochures, photographs, souvenirs or anything else connected with your holiday that you'd like to bring along.'

A buzz of genuine interest ran round the class.

'This should be fun,' Miss Walker had promised. 'We shall all be taken on a tour of a rich variety of places. It will be almost as good as the holiday programmes on television.'

Everyone except Charlie agreed with this. In fact, the idea had awakened lots of excitement and enthusiasm, and by break-time people were already discussing which holidays they would choose.

Lydia Davis was reminding everyone that last February she had been to the Carnival in Tenerife and had brought home carnival masks and favours, as well as a special newspaper edition filled with coloured carnival pictures. Better still, her dad had filmed the whole parade and there were hopes that the class would be able to see that as part of the project.

Simon Lee had been skiing in Austria and was planning to wear his skiing outfit on the day he gave his talk. He said he had brought back a wooden model of an Austrian chalet which played two different tunes depending on whether you opened the front or back doors.

'And,' he added importantly, 'we had apple strudel every day. My mum got the recipe and I'll ask her to make us some when it's my turn.'

Becky Adamson claimed snootily that you couldn't really talk about a place properly

until you had been to it at least three times. She had been to Spain three times, and had a bullfight poster and some castanets to prove it, besides a real Spanish doll that cost a fortune, with layers and layers of lovely, silver-lacy frills all down her long frock.

'Trust her!' thought Charlie mutinously. He didn't like Becky Adamson's constant boasting, and felt she ought to be taken down a peg or two. The others didn't seem to mind, though; they were all too taken up with their own ideas to bother complaining about Becky.

Even Joe Spriggs, who had six brothers and sisters, had been to the Lake District on a camping holiday, had sailed on lake Windermere, hiked over Honister Pass and found a magnificent fossil which he'd already shown Miss Walker twice.

In fact everyone had been somewhere really special at some time or another – everyone except Charlie. One-parent families cannot afford such luxuries as holidays, and Charlie knew with miserable certainty that he was going to hate the whole project. When his turn came to speak, unless he talked about 'my holiday at home', he would have nothing to say. The rest of the class would jeer and

Miss Walker would be bitterly disappointed in him.

It was all his own fault, of course, for putting his hand up in the first place, but he hadn't realised just then how much trouble he was in for.

The trouble was starting already.

'What about your holiday, Charlie?' someone asked.

'You'll have to wait and see,' mumbled Charlie. 'Mine's a surprise.'

For two days Charlie walked around in a black depression. He felt cross with his mother because she had never taken him on holiday, and cross with himself for feeling cross with his mother who, after all, did the best she could in very difficult circumstances. She worked hard at the dry-cleaner's and tried to give Charlie little treats whenever possible. Little treats such as a rented video film on a Saturday night, or a trip to the cinema with a bag of popcorn; treats which his friends would all take very much for granted. In fact, they wouldn't regard such things as treats at all, just part of everyday living. Charlie couldn't help feeling that life was most unfair.

And then, in the very depths of his despair, Charlie had a brainwave. He would invent a holiday. He would make up all the things he had done on that holiday and pretend it had all happened a long time ago, so that nobody would ever be able to check up on him.

'That's cheating!' his conscience whispered. But Charlie was past caring.

TWO

Planning to Cheat

The next Saturday morning Charlie went round to the travel agent's shop. First he browsed in the window at all the colourful posters and brochures there. Which country should he choose? Norway? Australia? The Bahamas? Thailand? What about a visit to the Grand Canyon or the Pyramids? It was going to be a very hard decision.

Then suddenly he spotted the answer to his problem! Disneyland Paris Theme Park! Why hadn't he thought of it before? That was a holiday near enough to home for people to believe him, yet important and colourful enough to make a really super talk.

Strangely enough, not one member of the class had been to Disneyland Paris Theme Park, though they all mentioned frequently that they would love to go. If he chose that

PARIS
AMSTER
VIENE
ROME

for his subject everyone would be interested, even envious, especially Becky Adamson.

Before he could change his mind, Charlie hurried into the travel agent's. There were three assistants, all of them busy on their computers checking up details of holidays for anxious customers. Charlie felt they were all concentrating far too hard to notice him. He sidled over to a long rack of holiday brochures and picked out the Disneyland Paris Theme Park one. He was just about to stuff it inside his anorak when a voice behind him asked:

'Now, young man, can I help you?'

The manager of the shop had suddenly

appeared from nowhere and was leaning over Charlie with a suspicious look on his face.

Charlie's cheeks turned pink.

'I – er – I was just getting one of your Disneyland Paris Theme Park brochures. My mum couldn't come because she's working.'

'I see! Just taken the one brochure, have you? We don't want all our shelves stripped bare, just for you to go cutting pictures out. Paper's very precious, not to mention expensive.'

The manager was remembering an occasion not so long ago when a whole

classful of pupils from a nearby school had
descended on the shop like a swarm of locusts
and carried off no less than two hundred
brochures between them, to use, he had later
discovered, in a school collage competition.

Charlie held out the brochure and
unzipped his anorak to show there was
nothing inside it but his shirt and himself.

'All right then, off you go. And tell your
mother I'll be looking out for her coming in
to book her tickets. I'll give her my personal
attention.'

Looking out for her? Did this mean the

man knew Charlie's mum? If he did, that could turn Charlie's whole plan into a disaster, because if Mrs Lyle got to hear what he was up to, she would never let him do it. Charlie could almost hear her voice.

'That's cheating!' she would tell him, as if he didn't know. 'You're supposed to talk about something you've actually done.'

Great! When all he had actually done was to explore the meagre possibilities of the local playing-field or set out on a mammoth expedition taking the washing to the launderette.

THREE

Burgled!

However, for the moment all was well. Mrs
Lyle was still at work, and Charlie sat at the
kitchen table with the brochure propped in
front of him, scribbling down the basic idea?
for his talk.

'First we went to the airport. Then we fle
to Paris. Then we went to Disneyland Par
Theme Park on the Metro.'

No; wait a minute! He crossed out 'on
Metro' because he wasn't sure if it wen
far as Disneyland Paris Theme Park w
was a long way outside Paris. He mu
careful not to make any give-away mis'
so he wrote 'on the bus' instead. Th
added: 'We paid our money and went ii

Yes; and then what?

Charlie stared forlornly at the pic'
the brochure. There was a bewilder

attractions, from a fairytale castle to a giant-sized Mickey Mouse, but he couldn't quite imagine how he would have felt about these things if he'd seen them for real.

He was trying so hard that he almost chewed through the end of his pencil. After a while, he wrote:

'We walked about a bit, then we had something to eat.'

This was all very well, but it could have happened anywhere. He wasn't telling what Disneyland Paris Theme Park was really like. How could he, when he didn't know?

Suddenly Charlie remembered Dulcie Evans, next-door-but-two. She was only six, but she had been to Disneyland Paris Theme Park once. She could tell him all about it.

Nimbly as a shoplifter, Charlie fled the house and hurried round to Dulcie's, forgetting, in his impatience, to lock the front door.

Dulcie was playing in the garden with her friend Fiona. They were making a picnic for their dolls, setting out broken bits of potato crisps, peanuts and dolly-mixtures on the tiny plastic plates of a doll's teaset, and pouring water into tiny cups.

'Hi, Dulcie!' called Charlie, somewhat over-cheerfully. He did not normally consort

with people under the age of nine.

Dulcie looked up and frowned. 'You can't come in!' she pouted.

'I don't want to, thanks. I just want to ask you about your trip to Disneyland Paris Theme Park, because I might be going. Did you have a good time?'

'It was all right,' Dulcie admitted grudgingly, 'but it rained all the while and I got sick from eating too many doughnuts.'

'But what was it LIKE?'

'I've forgotten.'

'She was only four when she went,' Fiona pointed out.

'Well, she must remember something. What did you do, Dulcie? Did you go on the rides? Did you see Mickey Mouse?'

'No! My dad carried me and I fell asleep.'

'What, all the time?' Charlie couldn't believe his ears. Fancy going to Disneyland Paris Theme Park and then falling asleep!

'Why don't you stop pestering?' grumbled Fiona. 'I don't know why you're bothering us anyway. You'll soon find out what it's like when you get there.'

'I need to know NOW! Surely you can remember some of it, Dulcie?' pleaded Charlie.

'Leave her alone!' cried Fiona crossly.

'Yes, go away! Anyway,' Dulcie declared, 'my doll's eaten all her picnic now. She wants to go to bed.'

'So does mine,' agreed Fiona.

They picked up their dolls and went indoors, leaving poor Charlie leaning unhappily on the gate – until Mrs Evans came out and asked him not to swing on it as he might damage the hinges.

Charlie wandered back home, convinced by now that even cheating was not easy. He could never write about a place he hadn't been to. He needed a real, personal experience. What should he do, then? At that moment he felt this to be the biggest problem in his life . . . but he was wrong! A much bigger problem – a truly gigantic problem – was about to present itself.

When Charlie reached home he noticed that the front door was ajar. Surely he had locked it? Perhaps his mum had come home early? If she had, then either she was ill or she had lost her job. Filled with sudden anxiety, Charlie dashed into the house.

The living-room was in a terrible mess! Drawers were pulled out and their contents

strewn everywhere; chairs were overturned; a flower-pot had been thrown down, spilling damp soil across the carpet; and worst of all, the television set was missing!

They'd been burgled!

Charlie remembered now that he had been so keen to sort out his holiday problem that he hadn't locked the door. He had even left the key behind on the kitchen table, and he saw to his horror that the key had now disappeared. He daren't think what his mother was going to say, for he knew that the burglary was all his fault.

'That's what comes of trying to cheat!' he told himself bitterly.

FOUR

Uncle Chris Has a Brainwave

When Mrs Lyle heard the news she came straight home from the dry-cleaner's. Needless to say, she was dreadfully upset. Quite apart from all the mess and the loss of her property, she was worried now about future security. Would the burglar come back again? He had actually taken their door key! Would he turn up in the middle of the night and murder them both in their beds?

Mrs Lyle felt she needed a bit of moral support. She telephoned the police, of course, but she also sent a message to her brother, Charlie's Uncle Chris, who was their only living relative. Uncle Chris worked on an oil rig off the coast of Scotland, but at present he was on leave, staying at a hotel in Edinburgh. They had just received a postcard from him with a picture of the Edinburgh hotel on it.

As she had no telephone herself, Mrs Lyle left her next-door neighbour's telephone number at the hotel reception desk, together with an urgent request for Uncle Chris to get in touch with her as soon as possible, as there was a bit of a crisis on at home.

Two police officers came to the house, a man and a woman. One of the first things they suggested was that Mrs Lyle should have the locks changed so that the burglar could not use her key. They also suggested having a burglar alarm fitted, but Mrs Lyle said she could not afford one.

Then the officers questioned Charlie. What time had he left the house? How long had he been away? Had he noticed anyone near the house when he came back? At first Charlie said he hadn't, but then he did remember seeing a man getting into a van which was parked a little way up the street. The man had been carrying a television set.

'OUR television set!' thought Charlie, with sudden shock.

That man must have been the burglar, though of course Charlie could never have guessed at the time.

'Can you describe him?'

Charlie did his best, and when he really

concentrated it was surprising what he could remember. The man had been wearing a green anorak and a blue woolly cap. He was also wearing gloves. Black leather gloves that came halfway to his elbows, like the sort motorcyclists wore. Charlie found he could even remember the make and colour of the van, though not its registration number.

'Well done, Charlie!' The officers assured him he'd been very helpful.

'You never know, your information might just be the vital bit that helps us to catch him.'

Charlie was not consoled. Nothing he did now could ever make up for his first mistake in leaving the door unlocked.

A little while later, while Charlie was making his mother a cup of tea, the doorbell rang and there was Uncle Chris standing large as life on the doorstep! As he had already hired a car for his holiday, Uncle Chris had decided to drive to his sister's straight away to find out what was going on.

'I didn't like the sound of your "bit of a crisis" and I didn't fancy listening to some garbled tale on next door's 'phone, so here I am.'

Mrs Lyle was very glad to see him, though

she kept on protesting that she hadn't expected him to interrupt his holiday.

'I just wanted you to telephone,' she explained. 'I needed somebody to talk to.'

'Well, now you've got somebody, so talk away!' laughed Uncle Chris. 'As for my hoiday, I've seen as much as I want to of Edinburgh now, and I quite fancied finishing off my leave here. In fact, I was going to come along anyway in a couple of days and surprise you.'

Charlie thought it was great to have Uncle Chris on the spot, for he sorted everything out in record time. He found a locksmith and dealt with Mrs Lyle's insurance policy. He even bought some stain-remover for the carpet where soil from the smashed plant had been trodden in. Best of all, he rang the television hire firm, who immediately sent along another set. As a smoother of rough paths and a solver of problems there was no one better than Uncle Chris.

It was not surprising, then, that Charlie should eventually pluck up courage to mention his own private problem. At breakfast next morning, when Mrs Lyle had gone off to work, Charlie explained about the school holiday project, and all the wonderful results the rest of the class were bound to come up with.

'I need a proper holiday to talk about,' Charlie finished gloomily. 'So I thought maybe I could talk about yours. You could tell it me while it's still fresh in your mind.'

'My stay in Edinburgh? Well, sure I could tell you about it, but that's not the same as experiencing something yourself. Suppose you get asked questions at the end?'

Horror! Questions were something Charlie had never thought of. Becky Adamson was sure to ask him one, and Miss

Walker, too. He almost made up his mind to go along to Miss Walker and confess.

Uncle Chris looked thoughtful for a minute. Then he declared: 'Hey, I've got a much better idea!'

Charlie looked up in sudden hope. Uncle Chris was rich and he still had another week's leave. 'You mean – you'll take me on a real holiday? Back to Edinburgh? Or London. We could go to London, Uncle Chris. Or Disneyland Paris Theme Park. How about that?'

Uncle Chris laughed. 'Now, just a minute! You know very well you can't go gadding off in the middle of the school term. My idea's even better than that, and it can all be fitted in on Sunday. A holiday is a new and completely different experience, and that's what you're going to have.'

Charlie's face fell. For one wonderful moment his hopes had been raised, but one day didn't seem much of a holiday, especially a boring old Sunday when everything was usually closed, and he was beginning to think that this time his hitherto wonderful Uncle Chris had let him down.

But Uncle Chris said: 'Trust me! If you do as I say, then with a bit of luck, you'll give the best holiday talk of the lot. In fact, you'll knock 'em for six!'

When Sunday came Uncle Chris made Charlie get up early. He would not explain where they were going, but he insisted that Charlie should put on his wellington boots and his oldest clothes. That sounded even less like a holiday to Charlie, but as there was little alternative he did as he was told.

'Are we going in your car?'

'No.'

'On the bus?'

'No.'

'On the train, then?'

'No. We're going on foot.'

On FOOT? What sort of a holiday was that? By this time Charlie felt completely disillusioned.

Uncle Chris packed a haversack with several items, including his binoculars, and at last they started out.

It was a fine, sunny morning as they strode away from the village and up a long, winding, muddy lane towards Beecher's farm.

'I used to go to school with Sam Beecher,' Uncle Chris explained. 'He hadn't much of a head for figures, but he was always a wizard with animals. Still is.'

Sam Beecher was obviously expecting them. He met them at the farmyard gate and

took them first of all into the farmhouse for refreshments. Mrs Beecher had just baked some gingerbread which smelt delicious.

After that, they started out on a tour of the farm. First they went to the hen-run and Mr Beecher let Charlie feed the hens with corn. He showed Charlie how to scatter the corn in great handfuls. At first, Charlie was nervous of the hens, who came squawking towards him in large numbers. But he soon realised that they were not interested in him; only in their dinner. In the end he grew so brave that he actually picked one hen up whilst he was walking around collecting lovely brown eggs in a basin.

Next came the lambs. They were only days old, but already they could leap and skip and make funny bleating noises. One of them was a poor little thing which had lost its mother, and Charlie was allowed to feed it from a baby's bottle. He felt very important looking after the lamb which could not look after itself. In fact, he could have played with the lambs all day, but there were so many other things to see.

After a scrumptious home-made lunch, Charlie carried a bucket of food-scraps out to the pig-sty and emptied it over the wall for the hungry pigs. There were seven little piglets too, and one of them was so small it was constantly being trampled on by the others. Twice Charlie had to lift it to safety. He grew quite fond of that little piglet and hoped he would come back and see it again.

Later on, he watched Mrs Beecher milk a cow. She promised Charlie that if he came regularly back to the farm at weekends and in school holidays she would one day teach him to milk cows himself. Charlie had already decided that he would visit the farm as often as the Beechers would let him.

The crowning glory of the afternoon came when Charlie was actually lifted up on to a horse's back, fitted out with a crash helmet and given a careful ride. The horse was called Brandy. Charlie had never ridden a horse before, but it was wonderful! He wasn't a bit afraid of Brandy; in fact, he wanted to go faster; to canter and even to gallop. But of course the grown-ups would not let him. Not yet. But he could always come back again for another ride, couldn't he?

There were lots of birds around on the farm land, which was why Uncle Chris had brought his binoculars. They spent some time bird-watching from the shelter of some bushes at the end of a field. They saw a robin, thrushes, a magpie and even, in one exciting moment, a brightly-coloured kingfisher swooping down towards the river.

'There's an owl in the barn as well,' Mr Beecher told them, 'but he's asleep just now.'

Charlie grew so interested in the birds that Uncle Chris promised to lend him a book with pictures of all the different kinds, so that he could start to recognise them for himself.

'I never knew there was so much to do, only twenty minutes' walk from our house!' admitted Charlie. The day had passed very quickly and already it was time to go home.

'When can I come back?'

'Whenever you like,' promised Mr Beecher. 'We might have turned you into a good little helper by next harvest time.'

Charlie didn't stop talking all the way home, and when he got there he talked even faster, telling his mother all about his day.

'Well,' grinned Uncle Chris, 'I reckon it's time you got some of that down on paper.'

FIVE

Last-Minute Blow

Charlie composed his talk. He wrote it all out on four sheets of paper. He guessed his spelling wasn't up to much, but he certainly had plenty to say.

'A farm holiday is the best holiday ever,' his talk began.

'You're not going to READ it, are you?' asked Uncle Chris, hearing Charlie practise. 'Talks are better as talks. You should learn it off by heart.'

Charlie stared in dismay at the four packed pages.

'I'll never learn it in time! My turn comes up on Wednesday.'

Yet he found that after all he didn't need to learn his talk word for word. As soon as he got started, he remembered so clearly all the things he had done at the farm that he could describe them without hesitation. It was real, and it had only just happened, so it was all fresh in his mind.

When Monday came, Charlie rushed eagerly off to school, much to the amazement of his mother. He could hardly wait for Wednesday to come, when it would be his turn to give the 'holiday' talk.

At last the great day arrived. The class sat expectantly, especially Becky Adamson who had already informed everyone that Charlie Lyle was about to cheat.

'My mum says he's never been on a holiday in his life,' she told the class. 'He'll have to make it all up. And when he's finished, I'm going to tell Miss Walker that he's cheated.'

'Then you're a rotten sneak, Becky Adamson,' cried Lydia Davis. 'Anyway, I'll bet Charlie HAS been on holiday. He put his hand up like everyone else.'

The count-down was over. Charlie walked out to the front of the class with a huge, happy grin on his face. This was his moment of triumph. He was just about to begin his talk and enjoy that triumph when the classroom door opened and the head teacher, Mr Farley, popped his head in to ask Charlie to come along to his office right away.

'But sir — !'

'Right away, I said, Charles! And that

means NOW, this very instant.'

Charlie groaned quietly to himself. All that work, and now he had lost his chance.

There were two people waiting in Mr Farley's office. Charlie recognised them at once as the two police officers who had been investigating his burglary. They had some photographs with them, which they wanted Charlie to look at. Some of the photographs were of people, and some were of vans. Did Charlie recognise any of them? He looked at the photographs carefully, and at last he was able to pick out both the burglar and his van, to the great delight of everyone including Mr Farley.

'Well done, Charles!' cried the Head. 'You have just helped to put an end to this village's reign of terror. Nineteen break-ins in the past two weeks, including my house, the post office and the travel agent's.'

'Can I go back to my class now, sir?' Charlie enquired anxiously. 'I'm supposed to be giving a talk.'

However, by the time he reached the classroom Miss Walker had asked another child to take over, and when that child had finished talking there was no more time left for Charlie.

'YOU had a lucky escape, then, didn't you?' sneered Becky Adamson. 'Or timed it beautifully, I don't know which. We all know you were going to cheat.'

'Well,' retorted Charlie, 'I'd rather cheat than go around saying nasty, horrible things about everybody.'

SIX

Rewards Galore!

Saturday came, and it was time for Uncle Chris to go back to his oil rig.

'No more holidays until next summer,' he mourned. 'But I've got four weeks to come then, right in the middle of your school holidays. So why don't we all go away together for a few days, the three of us? Where was it you fancied, Charlie? Disneyland Paris Theme Park?'

'Oh, we can't do that, Chris!' Mrs Lyle protested. 'Just think how much it would cost.'

'Well, I hope I'm allowed to treat my family once in a while, and don't forget you're the only family I've got! I just wish I'd thought of it sooner. Leave it to me, and I'll see that the whole thing's fixed up.'

Charlie should have felt thrilled, but he

seemed unusually quiet. After a while he said: 'Does it have to be Disneyland Paris Theme Park? Or could we have a holiday on a farm somewhere?'

Uncle Chris seemed highly amused. 'All right, I'll tell you what. You go along to the travel agent's and ask about farm holidays. He'll give you a brochure, then you can pick out the farm you want and send the details on to me.'

On Sunday Charlie was up with the dawn chorus. He spent the whole day at Beecher's farm again and thoroughly enjoyed every minute of it. He felt genuinely keen to tell his friends so that they could think about going to a farm as well. A pity he had lost the chance of his talk. He would have to do the best he could at break-time.

On Monday morning came the last of the talks. It was Simon Lee's turn, and as promised his mother drove up with the back seat of the car covered in apple strudels. Everybody enjoyed that except Becky Adamson who said the apples tasted sour. Charlie wondered what she would have found to grumble about in his talk if he had ever had the chance to present it. Well, he would never know.

Ah, but then Miss Walker reminded the class that Charlie had missed out.

'I hadn't forgotten. Your turn tomorrow, Charlie,' she smiled, and Charlie's spirits rose. What's more, he had had a brilliant idea for something to bring along. He would ask Mr Beecher if he could borrow the little piglet and take it to school in a basket.

He ran straight off to the farm after school and made his request.

'Oh, I don't know about that,' said Mr Beecher. 'It'd scare the poor little thing half to death. And anyway you might lose him. He wouldn't just sit still all day, you know. He'd be out of that basket the first chance he got.'

Charlie was very disappointed. He had thought it was such a brilliant idea. Having already explained to Mr Beecher about the holiday talks, Charlie had expected him to understand and co-operate.

'I'll tell you what you CAN do, though,' said Mr Beecher thoughtfully. 'You can ask your teacher if she'll bring the whole class up here to have a look round. I'm sure they'd enjoy it, and it would be good for them to see what goes on.'

So Charlie Lyle ended up covered in glory, in more ways than one. Not only was his talk declared the best by a beaming Miss Walker,

but the whole class was thrilled at the idea of
a visit to the farm. All except Becky
Adamson, who complained that it was bound
to be muddy and smelly. When the rest of
the class shouted her down, she retaliated by
claiming that Charlie Lyle had cheated after
all.

'Beecher's farm's only a few miles up the
lane. I don't call that going on holiday.'

At this point Miss Walker intervened,
pointing out that nobody had said the holiday
had to be long-distance, or to last more than a
day. And in fact, Charlie had packed more
new experiences into his one day than many
of the others had into a whole week.

'That was the whole point of the exercise,'
Miss Walker declared. 'Now let's have no
more unpleasantness, please.'

When the day for the farm visit came, Becky was mysteriously absent but the rest of the class had a wonderful time. Some of them admitted that they envied Charlie his regular visits there, especially his rides on Brandy. Even the ones who were not too keen on animals thought the day had been a big improvement on ordinary lessons. In fact, Charlie was the hero of the hour.

To crown it all, Charlie's photograph was in the local newspaper as the lad who helped the police to track down a burglar. There was half a column of writing underneath which Charlie scanned anxiously, but he was relieved to see that it did not mention his forgetting to lock the door. The reporter had described him as 'observant and sensible' and had said that if everyone behaved like that, the crime rate would soon go down.

As if that were not enough glory for one term, there was a further surprise to follow. When Charlie went in to the travel agent's to pick up some information about farm holidays, the manager spotted him and immediately called him into his office.

Charlie sprang to his own defence.

'I haven't taken any brochures,' he declared. 'Honest! You can search me if you like.'

The manager laughed. 'It's all right, son. I'm not worried about brochures at the moment. But the thing is, you've saved me a journey, because I was going to come along to your house tonight.'

Charlie stared in dismay. Then he remembered he had told the manager that he and his mother were going to Disneyland Paris Theme Park. The manager had said he would look out for Mrs Lyle coming in to book the holiday. So because she hadn't been in, he must be intending to go to the house to ask her about it.

'Listen, mister, I can explain everything . . .' Charlie began hurriedly.

'No need. The police have already explained.'

Charlie didn't like the sound of that. He was the sort of lad who got himself into trouble without even noticing. What had he done now?

'Don't look so worried!' laughed the manager. 'All I want to do is give you your reward.'

What reward? Now young Charlie was completely flabbergasted. Then he remembered that the burglar had broken into the travel agent's as well, and stolen the entire day's

takings plus lots of airline tickets and all the foreign currency they had on the premises. The parent travel firm had offered a reward for any information leading to the capture of the burglar.

'There you are, then! One reward as agreed. And jolly well deserved!'

The manager handed over a bulging envelope.

Bemused, Charlie took the envelope and turned it over in his hand as if it were an object from outer space. He didn't know what to say.

'Well, go on; open it!'

The manager produced a letter-opener, and at last Charlie was able to see what was inside the envelope.

Two airline tickets to Paris, two hotel reservations for a week, and two tickets to Disneyland Paris Theme Park!

'It's a good thing your mother hadn't made her booking yet!' the manager grinned.

'You mean – these are for us?'

Charlie was so excited that he almost forgot to ask for the farm holiday brochures.

At school the next day, Charlie made a point of seeking out Becky Adamson and letting her know that this summer he was going to have not one holiday but two.

'So what?' retorted Becky, 'We have two holidays every year.'

Charlie smiled. 'Well, I bet you won't have half as much fun on yours as I will.'

Hazel Townson

Charlie the Champion Liar

To keep face after a disappointing birthday, Charlie Lyle pretends he's been given a video camera. But he quickly finds that this one small lie draws him into a whole series of lies when someone suggests he makes a video of a PE display . . .

A wonderfully funny story by a master storyteller, whose books have been previously described by Stephanie Nettell as "rollicking rough and tumble fun".

"an amusing story with a bit of a moral . . ."
Junior Bookshelf

Hazel Townson

The Peckthorn Monster

'There's a monster in Peckthorn Woods!'

Suddenly the peaceful life of the whole village is threatened. No one knows what to do – except young Peter and his sister, Katy. Ignoring adult warnings, the children set off to the woods in seach of the monster – but they are in for a great many shocks and surprises.

A delightfully zany comedy by the author of the best-selling *Charlie the Champion Liar*.

"Monster fun."
Gloucestershire Echo

Jeff Brown

Flat Stanley

Stanley Lambchop is just a normal healthy boy, though since an enormous noticeboard fell on him while he was asleep he's been only half an inch thick!

Stanley finds he can now squeeze under doors, be lowered down a grating and even be posted in an envelope to California.

A hilarious story, now a classic.

Patrick Skene-Catling

The Chocolate Touch

John Midas is a normal, average sort of boy –
until he finds an old coin in the road. He uses it
to buy a very special box of chocolates. It
contains the most chocolaty chocolate John
Midas has ever eaten – but it leaves him with a
gift that could be a dream come true . . . or
a nightmare. Everything he touches turns to
chocolate!

"A brilliantly told story . . . Highly recommended . . ."
Books for Keeps

The sequel to *The Chocolate Touch*, *John Midas and
the Radio Touch* is also available from Mammoth.

Anne Fine

Bill's
New Frock

When Bill Simpson woke up on Monday morning, he found he was a girl . . . Forced off to school in a frilly pink dress, Bill discovers one of the worst days of his life is about to begin . . .

Baffled by the way things are just different for girls, Bill falls headlong into trouble. As the amazing day drags on, Bill's new frock becomes dirtier and tattier. How will it all end for him – or her?

Winner of the Smarties Award, Highly Commended for the Carnegie Medal and winner of the Nottinghamshire Book Award.

Anne Fine

The Country Pancake

Like an angel, Miss Mirabelle stepped into the lives of the children of Wallisdean Park School. Enchanting she may be, but Miss Mirabelle still ends up in Big Trouble. Lancelot, her adoring champion, comes up with the most original idea ever to save his damsel in distress. But it all depends on his beloved Flossie, the cow . . .

". . . entirely charming tale of an unconventional teacher, a suspicious head, an imaginative class and a co-operative cow."
Times Educational Supplement

Douglas Hill

The Voyage of Mudjack

Mudjack might never have left home if it hadn't been for the magic boat named Halyard. He might have stayed on his father's ferry boat forever, just going back and forth across the river. But, more than anything else, Mudjack wanted to see the sea. How could he resist Halyard's invitation to take him on a voyage?

In hot pursuit are Halyard's owner 'Bully' Bargepole, the river pirate chief, aided and abetted by Fenmire the magician . . .

A fairy tale of a wish come true by a master of fantasy.

"crisply written and engagingly illustrated."
Junior Bookshelf

Robert Swindells

The Siege of Frimly Prim

The children of Frimly Prim hear that their school is to be closed down and decide there's only one thing they can do; sixteen of the top class decide to occupy the school.

It's fun but it gets tricky until one very old lady and one little girl with a teddy bear come to the rescue.

By the winner of the Carnegie Medal.

"A splendidly funny story . . ."
Books for Keeps

A Selected List of Fiction from Mammoth

☐	7497 1421 2	**Betsey Biggalow is Here!**	Malorie Blackman	£2.99
☐	7497 0366 0	**Dilly the Dinosaur**	Tony Bradman	£2.99
☐	7497 0137 4	**Flat Stanley**	Jeff Brown	£2.99
☐	7497 0983 9	**The Real Tilly Beany**	Annie Dalton	£2.99
☐	7497 0592 2	**The Peacock Garden**	Anita Desai	£2.99
☐	7497 0054 8	**My Naughty Little Sister**	Dorothy Edwards	£2.99
☐	7497 0723 2	**The Little Prince (colour ed.)**	A. Saint-Exupery	£3.99
☐	7497 0305 9	**Bill's New Frock**	Anne Fine	£2.99
☐	7497 1718 1	**My Grandmother's Stories**	Adèle Geras	£2.99
☐	7497 2395 5	**Flow**	Pippa Goodheart	£2.99
☐	7497 0041 6	**The Quiet Pirate**	Andrew Matthews	£2.99
☐	7497 1930 3	**The Jessame Stories**	Julia Jarman	£2.99
☐	7497 0420 9	**I Don't Want To!**	Bel Mooney	£2.99
☐	7497 1496 4	**Miss Bianca in the Orient**	Margery Sharp	£2.99
☐	7497 0048 3	**Friends and Brothers**	Dick King Smith	£2.99
☐	7497 0795 X	**Owl Who Was Afraid of the Dark**	Jill Tomlinson	£2.99